MEL BAY'S
Flute PRIMER

By Lou Hittler

Flute Primer is a beginner's guide to the flute. The text is especially useful for the trial or rental period. Great emphasis has been placed in this text on sound fundamentals, embouchure, tone and other basic techniques. Upon completion of *Flute Primer* the student will be ready to enter into Mel Bay's *Flute Method.*

1 2 3 4 5 6 7 8 9 0

PARTS OF THE FLUTE

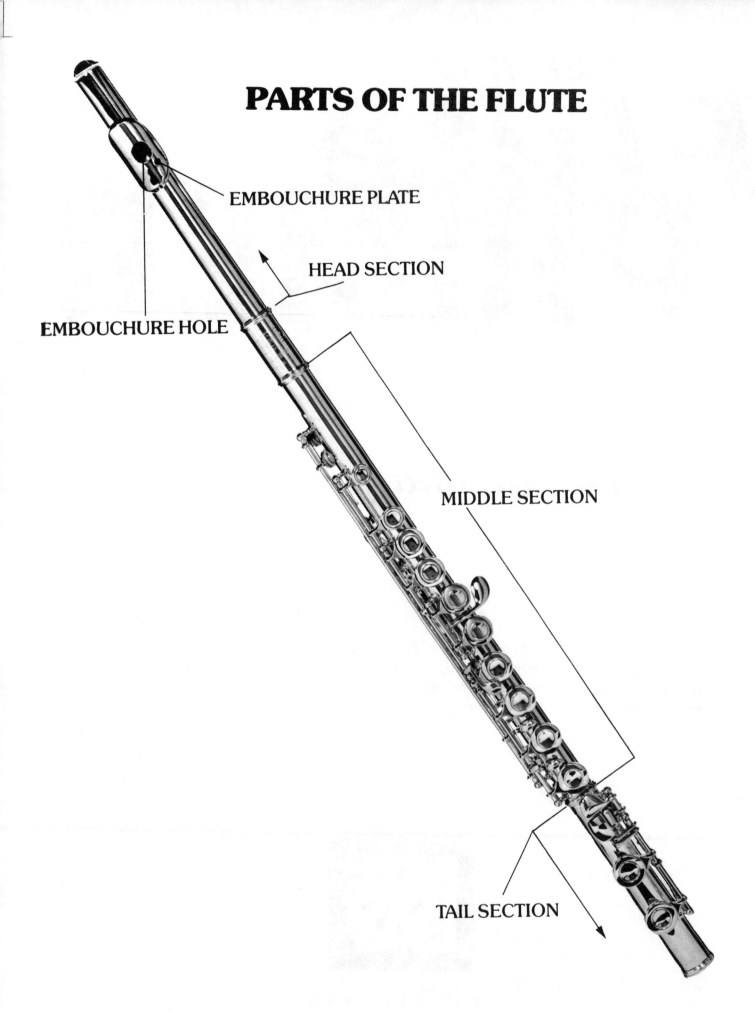

EMBOUCHURE PLATE

HEAD SECTION

EMBOUCHURE HOLE

MIDDLE SECTION

TAIL SECTION

FLUTE FINGERING CHART

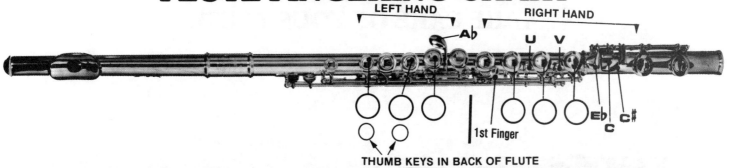

TO PLAY "G" NOTE, FOR EXAMPLE,

● INDICATES FINGER PLATE CLOSED
○ INDICATES FINGER PLATE OPEN
LETTERS INDICATE KEY TO BE DEPRESSED

Fig. 1. The first three finger plates are closed by the first three fingers of the *left* hand.

Fig. 2. The next three finger plates remain open.

Fig. 3. The *Eb key* is depressed with the little finger of the *right hand*.

Fig. 4. Thumb key is depressed with the left thumb.

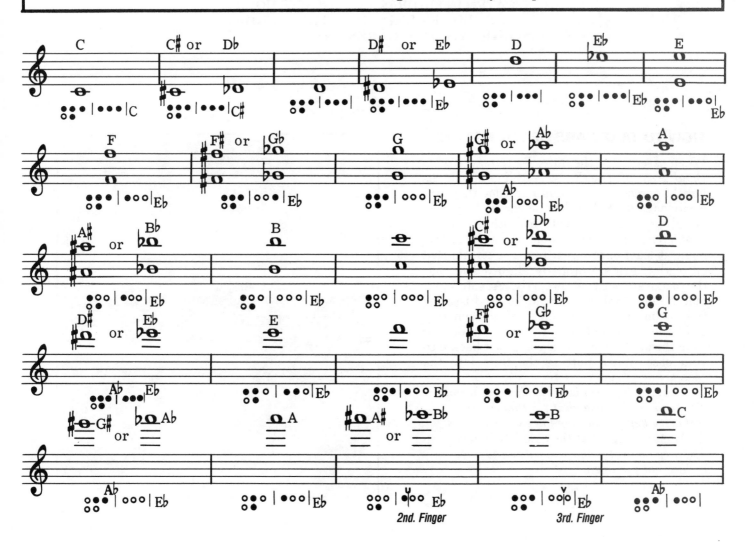

HOW TO ASSEMBLE AND
TAKE CARE OF YOUR FLUTE

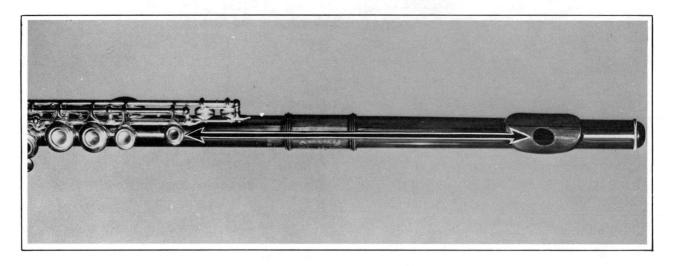

FIG. 5

PUT THE FLUTE TOGETHER AS INDI-
CATED IN FIGURES 5, 6, 7 & 8. THE HOLES
SHOULD BE ALIGNED AS THE ARROWS
INDICATE IN FIGURES 5 & 6.

HOW TO TAKE CARE OF YOUR FLUTE

When assembling the flute, *Be Careful Not to Bend Any of The Keys.* Vaseline should be lightly spread on the joints so that they will easily engage. A light key oil should be placed on all working parts with a toothpick and a competent repair man should check the instrument at least once a year to make certain that all of the keys are properly aligned and that the pads are seating properly. A soft cloth placed on a swab rod should be used to wipe the inside of the instrument after each use. This will clean out any remaining moisture from the instrument when you put it back into your case. When putting the flute into the case always make certain:

(1) That the flute is placed in the case properly. Never force the case shut for this could seriously bend or damage keys.

(2) Make certain that the case is securely fastened so that when you carry the flute it does not fall open.

FIG. 6

FIG. 7

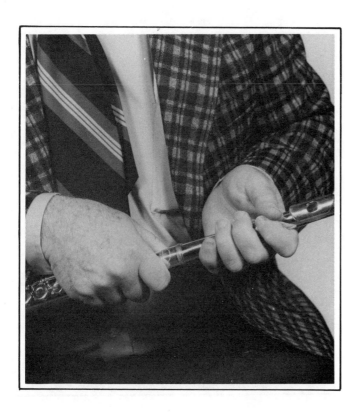

FIG. 8

How To Assemble The Flute

FIGURE 7

First, we will connect the tail section with the middle section of the flute. The bottom or tail section of the flute should lie in the palm of your right hand. Pressure will be applied when assembling by the thumb of your right hand resting on the post. The palm of the left hand should nestle the back of the middle section of the flute. Do not put your fingers on the keys. This should not be necessary. You should be able to get a firm grip without grabbing the keys. Never force the instrument together. Apply gentle pressure so as not to damage any working parts. Finally, line up the keys as shown in Figure 6.

FIGURE 8

To insert the mouthpiece section into the flute, rest the middle section in the right hand. The mouthpiece section should rest in the left hand. The embouchure hole should line up with the keys as shown in Figure 5.

5

HOW TO HOLD THE FLUTE

To hold the instrument properly, rest the flute above the third joint of the first finger of the left hand (see picture). Keep the fingers slightly arched above the keys that they are to manipulate. The little finger of the right hand should be on the Eb key. The thumb of the right hand is kept on the underneath side of the flute between the first and second finger of the right hand. Remember, the flute must be parallel to the lips. Keep the elbows slightly away from the body and remember to keep your body relaxed.

SIDE VIEW

PROPER SITTING POSITION

Observe the photograph showing proper sitting position when playing the flute. You will notice that the elbows are held out from the body in a loose manner so that your breathing may be free and easy. Do not slouch, sit in an upright position with the lower part of your back against the chair. Make certain that while you are sitting upright, you are not rigid.

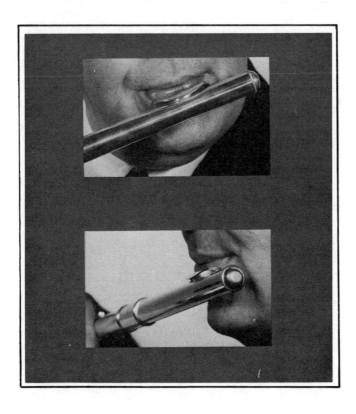

GETTING A TONE ON THE FLUTE
EMBOUCHURE

The embouchure is the positioning of the lips for playing your instrument. In producing a tone on the flute, the proper embouchure is extremely important. First, it is important to keep the mouth muscles relaxed. Use the muscles at the corner of the mouth for gaining the proper tension. The center of the lip should remain relaxed. At first, close your lips naturally, blowing a stream of air thru a small opening in the center. *Do Not* tense the center of the upper and lower lip. After experimenting with your lip positioning, place the tone hole or embouchure hole on the lower lip so that approximately one-third of the hole is covered by the lower red portion of the lip. Now blow gently as described above. After producing a clear sound, place the tongue against the upper teeth, retracting the tongue as you blow. This will allow the air column to start. This is similiar to saying "tu." It is also called "tonguing."

WHOLE NOTES, WHOLE RESTS, AND $\frac{4}{4}$ OR (COMMON) TIME

4/4 time gets four beats to the bar. A whole note (𝆸) gets four counts. (One and, two and, three and, four and.) A whole rest (▬) gets four full counts also. One and, two and, three and, four and.)

OUR FIRST NOTES

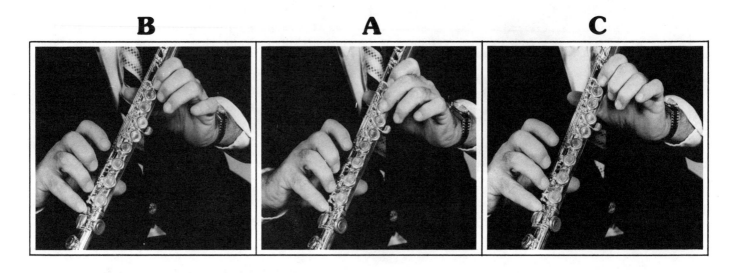

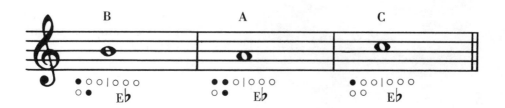

TIME TO PLAY

8

MORE NOTES

G F E

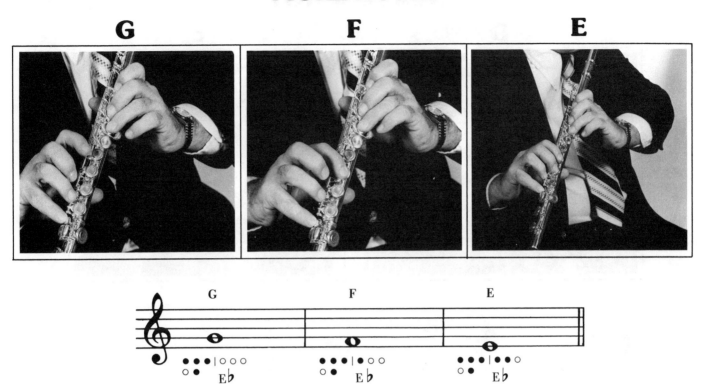

PLAY AGAIN

HALF NOTES, QUARTER NOTES AND BREATH MARKS

A half note (♩) gets two full beats. Count one and, two and.)

A quarter note (♩) gets one beat. (One and.)

Watch out for breath marks ('). A breath mark means to take a breath. Keep blowing out smoothly until time to breathe. Breathe deep and use your tongue to start each new note.

OUR FIRST SONG!

FOUR NEW NOTES

D

E

F

G

EXPLORING!

SAME SONG USING NEW NOTES

THE TIE

A tie looks like this (⌒). When a tie appears, tongue the first note and hold (do not tongue) the second note that it is tied to.

WHEN THE SAINTS GO MARCHING IN

$\frac{3}{4}$ TIME—DOTTED HALF NOTE

In 3/4 time we count three beats per measure. (one and, two and, three and.) Watch out for the dotted half note. ($\downarrow$.) A dotted half note gets three full beats. (One and, two and, three and.)

HOME ON THE RANGE

LONDON BRIDGE

A TISKIT A TASKET

B

C

BILLY BOY

GOING HOME

13

$\frac{2}{4}$ TIME

In 2/4 time we have two beats for each measure. (one and, two and.) Each quarter note gets full beat.

SKIP TO MY LOU

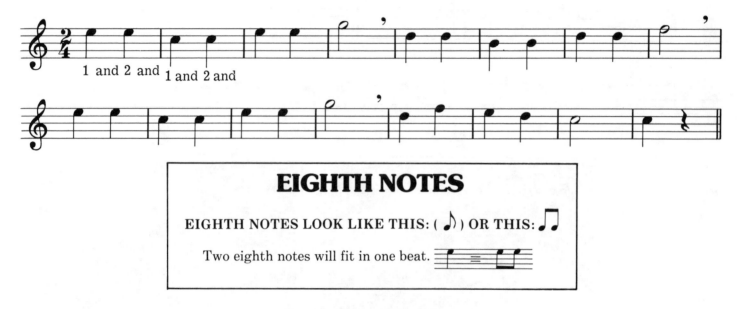

EIGHTH NOTES

EIGHTH NOTES LOOK LIKE THIS: (♪) OR THIS: ♫

Two eighth notes will fit in one beat.

SKIP AGAIN

YANKEE DOODLE

14

NEW NOTE B♭

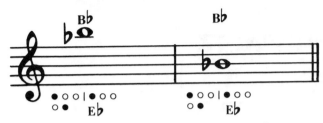

A FLAT LOOKS LIKE THIS —♭

A flat will lower a note $\frac{1}{2}$ tone. The flat is usually indicated at the beginning of each song and will make all B's flat unless otherwise indicated.

MARINES HYMN

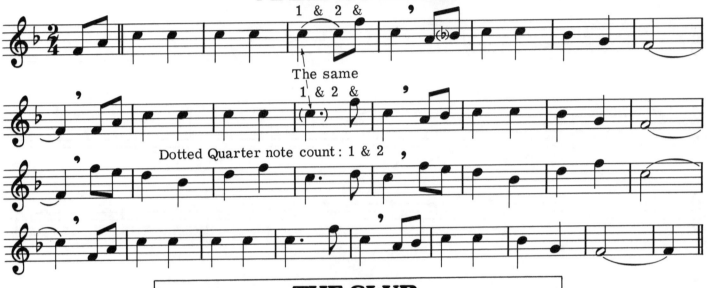

THE SLUR

A slur is a large bracket that connects one or more notes. When a slur occurs, tongue only the first note and merely finger all other notes under the slur.

AURA LEE

15

SOLOS

MERRY WIDOW WALTZ

REMEMBER:

In $\frac{3}{4}$ time we have 3 beats per measure.

Count: 1 and, 2 and, 3 and

STACCATO DANCE

Stacatto means short and is indicated by a dot over or under the note.

F#

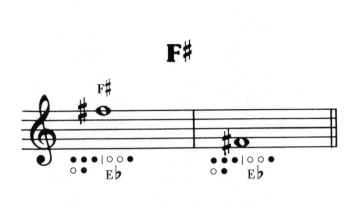

A SHARP LOOKS LIKE THIS — #

A sharp will raise a note $\frac{1}{2}$ tone. The sharp is usually indicated at the beginning of each song and will make all F's sharp unless otherwise indicated.

BLUE BELLS OF SCOTLAND

means all F's are sharped.

MORE STACCATO

EIGHTH REST GETS 1/2 BEAT — SAME AS EIGHTH NOTE.

Count : 1   &   2   &

"HIGH D"

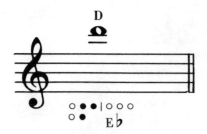

DYNAMICS

At this point, the songs will be marked for volume. *f* means loud. *mf* means medium loud. *mp* medium soft. *p* soft. *pp* very soft. ⟍ means get softer. ⟋ means get louder.

SKATERS' WALTZ

C#

E♭

ACCIDENTALS

An accidental is a sharp (♯), a flat (♭), or a natural (♮). The natural sign cancels out a sharp or a flat. When an accidental appears in front of a note like "C," for example, all remaining "C's" in that measure are affected. (If a sharp is placed before "C" in a measure, all remaining "C's" in that measure are played as C#!)

GOD OF OUR FATHERS

ACCIDENTAL SONG

O COME, ALL YE FAITHFUL

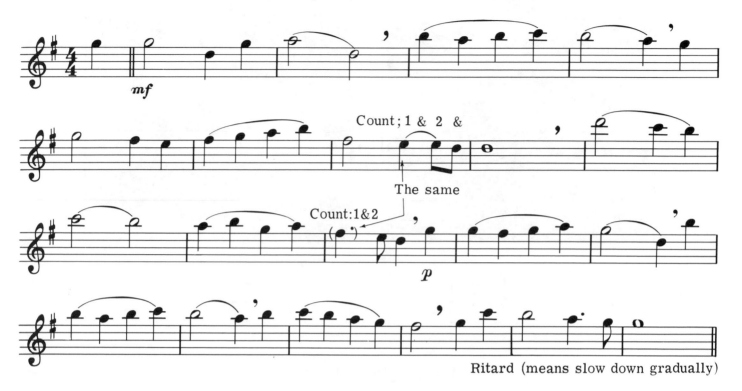

Count; 1 & 2 &

The same

Count:1&2

Ritard (means slow down gradually)

JINGLE BELLS

20

CAMPTOWN RACES

SKIPPING SONG

Playing slurred skips is good for lip development, so at this time we will play a song consisting of slurred, skipping intervals.

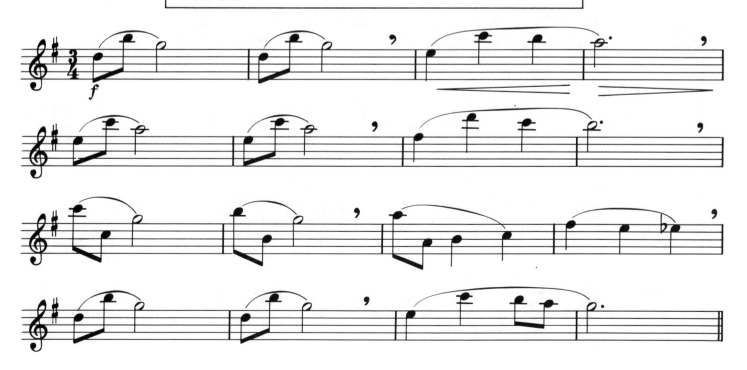

21

SWANEE RIVER

D.S. F.

When you see the letters D.S. in a piece, return back to this sign (𝄋). Then, continue until you reach the word "Fine" which means "The End."

MINUET

Fine

D.S. al Fine

MELODY

CAN CAN

WHEN THE SAINTS COME MARCHING IN

(In Three Keys)